TONY MILLIONAIRE'S

SOCK MONKEY™

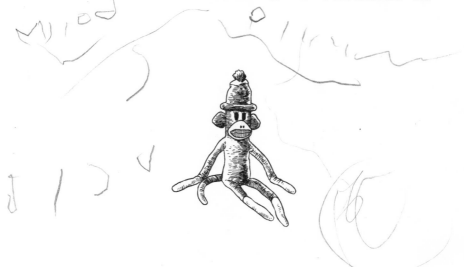

A Children's Book

Introduction by

J. OTTO SEIBOLD

DARK HORSE MAVERICK™

For Phoebe

---

editor
PHIL AMARA

book design
LIA RIBACCHI

art director, Dark Horse Maverick
CARY GRAZZINI

publisher
MIKE RICHARDSON

Thanks to Johnny Gruelle

TONY MILLIONAIRE'S
SOCK MONKEY, A CHILDREN'S BOOK

Published by
Dark Horse Comics, Inc.
10956 S.E. Main Street
Milwaukie, OR 97222

www.darkhorse.com
www.maakies.com

To find a comics shop in your area,
call the Comic Shop Locator Service
toll-free at 1-888-266-4226

First edition: November 2001
ISBN: 1-56971-549-1

1 3 5 7 9 10 8 6 4 2

PRINTED IN CANADA

O nce, many years ago, I had the pleasure of taking a plane ride to and from the printing of our very first children's picture book, Mr. Lunch Takes a Plane Ride. On the return trip, in a small Wisconsin airport, I encountered a shop that I shall never forget. Its shelves were stocked with an endless variety of the same object... sock monkeys! Two grannies ran the place, and they told me they were part of a larger group of grannies who had made all the monkeys. My mind swam with imagery... and I bought a monkey for my daughter at once. It became a dear member of the family, and has had maintenance stitching as regularly as the kids go to the dentist. Now, Tony Millionaire reveals more secrets of the sock monkey and other things made from the hands of grannies... enjoy!

—J. Otto Seibold

J. Otto Seibold is co-creator with Vivian Walsh of the Mr. Lunch books and Olive the Other Reindeer.

One day deep in the jungle, a monkey sat on a branch. He was normally a very happy monkey. He spent his time jumping from tree to tree with the other monkeys, and he had plenty of bananas and mangoes to eat. But today he wasn't interested in bananas or mangoes or any kind of food at all, for he had a terrible toothache! His cheek was swollen and he moaned and whimpered and held his head in his hands.

"My, that smarts!" he thought. "If only there was something I could do about it!" He reached a finger gingerly into his mouth and poked the sore tooth. "Why, it is loose!" he exclaimed, "I'll bet I could pull it out! " He held it between his fingers and gave a tug. If you have ever had a loose tooth, you will be able to imagine

"My, that smarts!" he thought.
"If only there was something I could do about it..."

his great relief when it easily popped out! He was so happy he did a somersault, nearly losing his balance, and he dropped the tooth, which tumbled and bounced down through the branches, and landed in a patch of moss, right under a beautiful wild orchid. The monkey was curious, and as he had never seen a tooth which was not still in someone's head, he climbed down to see how it looked.

"Hmm, it looks pretty much the same stuck in this moss as it does stuck in a monkey's mouth!" He was interrupted by a loud stomping and crashing in the jungle! He quickly scrambled up the tree as the bushes parted and there stood a big man with a big moustache and an even bigger butterfly net.

"Well, gentlemen!" thundered the big man, "We seem to be having no luck at

Odontoglossum O.

all in our search for butterflies today, we haven't uncovered even a solitary moth! But if you will look before you, you will see a prize greater than the most delicate swallowtail! This is a lovely specimen of *Odontoglossum O*, one of the rarest flowers to be found in all the world! It will make a splendid birthday present for my grand-daughter Ann-Louise! Rimperton! Bring me a bucket!" A rough-looking sailor with gold rings in his ears came huffing up the hill carrying a pail and a small shovel.

"Now dig carefully, Rimperton," said the captain, "these are very delicate flowers and they must be handled gently!"

Ann-Louise was very excited, as were all the people in the town. Her grandfather's ship had been spotted coming in to the harbor and she hadn't

There stood a big man with a big moustache...

seen him in a long time. She and her grandmother put on their best bonnets and hurried down to the wharf.

"I wonder if Grandfather has brought me something for my birthday?" Ann-Louise whispered to the soft ragdoll she held to her cheek.

"I certainly hope it is something pleasant!" replied the ragdoll. "The last time he returned from a voyage, he brought you a narwhal horn, and though it was a very interesting present, it wasn't exactly the kind of thing a girl hopes for on her birthday! In fact it was rather smelly!"

"Hello, little girl!" the captain shouted from the deck of the ship. "Did you miss me?" He was carrying a large sea chest on his shoulders, and she wondered what was inside.

Ann-Louise was very excited...

That night while Ann-Louise slept, the captain was busy up in his greenhouse. "I'd better put the orchid under this glass cloche, to keep it safe in this climate," he mumbled. "Won't Ann-Louise be surprised when she sees it! How lovely it is!" and he tiptoed off to bed.

Just behind the door stood a stuffed crow, not a dusty old taxidermy crow, but a soft fuzzy velvet crow with big yellow button eyes. He was whispering to his friends, the dolls.

"Did you see what the Captain brought in? It's some kind of a flower, some absurd plant from a far-away jungle."

"I heard him say it was an orchid," said the ragdoll.

"Orchid, my beak, it is another of his ridiculous collection of bizarre weeds which he is always fussing over."

The Glass Cloche

They climbed up the footstool and onto the bench where the orchid sat under its glass cover.

"It is weird I tell you, and I don't like it!" said the crow and he peered through the glass. "It looks like some kind of a beetle!"

Suddenly the orchid turned and stared straight into the crow's button eyes. The crow had seen many strange plants in the Captain's nursery, but up until now, none that had turned and none that had a face to turn!

"WOW!" exclaimed the crow, and he tumbled a complete somersault off the bench! In the process he knocked the dolls to the floor and worse than that he knocked the orchid to the floor, glass cover and all. What a crash!

"Very clumsy of you, Mr. Crow!" scolded the cornhusk doll. She was an

Suddenly the orchid turned!

elegant doll, very proper, and did not appreciate being jostled about.

"The next time you jump around bumping people off of workbenches and such, please have the courtesy to at least shout out a warning! Something along the lines of 'Hello, everyone! I'm planning on falling to the floor and bringing you all with me, watch out!' would be sufficient!"

She harrumphed as she straightened out her long cornhusk dress. The crow looked sheepish. The ragdoll spoke up, "Now, my dear, I'm sure he didn't mean it, did you Mr. Crow?"

"I'm quite sure I did not and I do apologize, ladies, but can you blame me? Did you see the vicious look on that flower? It was very alarming!"

"FLUKES AND FLAMES! What is all the consarn racket in here?" bellowed the

"Wow!" exclaimed the crow.

Captain, as he rushed into the greenhouse, swinging a broom. "Here I am, peacefully sleeping after a months-long voyage, only to find magical dolls and crows disturbing the tranquility of the night! Away with you!" and he swept them out the door! "Blasted come-to-life toys! If it wasn't for all the magic around here, we wouldn't be having all this infernal chaos all the time!"

His wife came in, dressed in a nightgown, "What's all this?" she asked, yawning. "Captain! Come back to bed!"

"Look at what those toys and dolls have been at again! I'll have to order a new glass cloche for this orchid, and it won't arrive for at least a week. Won't Ann-Louise be disappointed!"

"Why don't you just give her the flower without the jar?"

"Flukes and flames!"

"It is not a jar, my dear, it is a cloche! This orchid needs protection in this chilly climate, it is a tropical plant! And I can't very well make a present of an orchid under a tin bucket! Wouldn't that be a fine thing!"

"Now Captain, don't you worry about Ann-Louise, we'll find her a birthday present, mark my words!"

She noticed that the Captain was wearing his fine thick cotton socks, and that he was standing in the moss which had fallen to the floor with the orchid. "Careful, now, Captain, you are getting your socks all dirty!" She brought him downstairs and took off his socks.

"Hmm, these really are very nice socks," she thought. "Perhaps I can use them to sew a new doll for Ann-Louise's birthday present," and she sat down and started to work. First she cut one sock into

"Captain, you are getting your socks all dirty!"

strips, for the arms and legs. She carefully cut out the heel to use for a mouth. From the leftovers, she fashioned a hat.

"He looks like a monkey," she said, and she made a tail and sewed it on. Then she stuffed him with soft white cotton. She noticed something on the monkey's face. "What is this strange lump in the cloth? Something seems to have gotten stuck in the fabric of the sock, and I can't pull it out! Perhaps I'll just sew the mouth right over the lump." And she did...

Later that night the crow was creeping through the library. He often crept around the house at night, for he was naturally curious. He stopped short in his tracks, as he noticed that something was lurking in the shadows by the captain's desk. He peered into

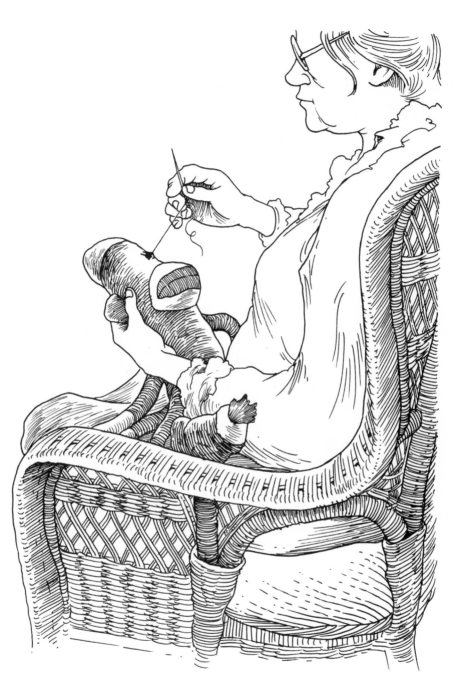

"He looks like a monkey," she said,
and she made a tail and sewed it on.

the darkness. Squinting, he realized that something was peering back at him, something with two eerie black eyes. He ran from the room and down the stairs!

"Ladies!" he squeaked to the dolls, who were up making tea. "I have seen the most hideous monster upstairs in the library! It is some kind of a moon-faced night-ape squatting camouflaged in a bush! It is horrible!"

"Come now, Mr. Crow," said the cornhusk doll. "There are no bushes in the library and I am sure I have never seen any sort of a night-ape anywhere in this house at all. Please have some tea and calm yourself."

"It was an ape I tell you! A freak of the highest order! A ghoul!"

"Now then! Enough of that!" scolded the ragdoll, "If you don't leave off with

"Camouflaged in a bush..."

your tall tales in the middle of the night, you'll wake Ann-Louise!"

"Don't you see, it's Ann-Louise I am most worried about! Who will protect her from these ghosts and goons if we do not! We must do something!"

"Well, the first goon we shall protect her from will be you, Mr. Crow! Now hush!" And the dolls hurried him off to bed.

The next morning the ragdoll came into the kitchen to help the cook make breakfast. She wasn't really much help, being so soft and small, but the cook liked to sit her up on a shelf and let her watch the business of the day. This morning, however, the ragdoll noticed an unusual guest in the kitchen. It was the crow, who was busy in the corner hanging a banana from a piece of string in the laundry chute.

"It was an ape, I tell you!"

"Now what are you up to, Mr. Crow?" asked the ragdoll. "Isn't it enough that you were up half the night carrying on about this wild monkey?"

"Listen to me, I will not be silenced!" exclaimed the crow, very flustered. "I intend to catch this monster if it is the last thing I do! I am setting a trap! I have hung this fruit here in the laundry chute where he is sure to notice it, and I have smeared the sill with butter. When he attempts to steal the fruit, he will slip on the butter and down he'll go, all the way to the basement, where I have placed a large cardboard box as a cage!"

"Mr. Crow! That is very dangerous! If the dog or the cat were to come in here and try to grab that banana, they could be badly hurt in the fall!"

"Don't be ridiculous, my dear, I have never seen a dog nor a cat who ever had

"I am setting a trap!"

any interest at all in a banana or any other kind of frui—!" The crow had been perched on the buttery sill while he was arguing with the ragdoll, wildly flapping his wings, and soon enough, he slipped in the butter and SWOOSH! down he went!

"Mr. Crow! Are you all right?" called the ragdoll down the long chute. The upstairs maid had thrown a big pile of laundry in that morning and it had stuck in the chute, so the crow had only a short fall onto a soft pile of dirty clothes. He picked himself up.

"Yes, I seem to be fine!" he brushed himself off. "But it is rather musty down here, what with all this dirty laundry. Could you please help me out?"

"I cannot, you are just out of reach! Wait here while I go for help!" and off she went.

He slipped in the butter and SWOOSH! down he went!

The crow was alone. It was dark down there, and he could just see the banana dangling over his head. The ragdoll had been gone for quite some time.

"What a fool I've been, plotting and building traps! And here I sit all alone in the dark, caught in a pit of my own design. Oh, where is that ragdoll, it's been awhile now, and I'm getting hungry. Even that old banana looks appetizing now, but I couldn't reach it if I tried. I'm frightened." He started to cry.

If you think he was frightened then, think of how frightened he was when he looked up and saw, framed in the door of the laundry chute, the head of the sock monkey silently staring down at him. He shrieked with terror! The monkey's head disappeared from the chute and the crow

The crow was alone...

curled himself into a ball and sobbed, trembling. After some time, he peered up again and this time he saw the monkey's tail slowly slithering down towards him. He opened his beak as wide as he could and just before he began to screech, he heard a voice from the kitchen.

"Grab hold of my tail, and I will pull you up!" Before he knew what he was doing, he wrapped his wingtips around the tail and felt himself being pulled up and out onto the kitchen floor! He jumped to his feet and ran as fast as ever he could all the way upstairs and back into his bed where he pulled the covers over his head and shivered for the rest of the morning. In fact he was so frightened that he missed his eleven o'clock tea and cookies, and he never missed that!

The Sock Monkey

L ater that afternoon, the crow was in the parlor talking to the dolls. "It was terrifying!" he explained, "That chimpanzee almost had me in his grasp! I barely escaped with my life!"

"See here now Mr. Crow, even if this monkey were real, there is no reason to be so afraid of him!" said the cornhusk doll. "You are being quite unreasonable, especially when you think of how you yourself came into this house!"

The crow looked angry. "Just what is that supposed to mean?!"

The dolls looked at the floor, sheepish. "Come on, out with it! I demand to know what you are talking about!" the crow shouted.

"Well, all right, if you must know," began the ragdoll. "When you first came

"I barely escaped with my life!"

to this house, you were just a plain old cloth crow. You were not alive like we all are now. You were like Robin."

Everyone turned toward Robin. Robin was a very beautiful doll, she had glass eyes and porcelain boots and a pretty white pinafore, but Robin was just a doll. She didn't walk around or talk or do any of the things that the other dolls did. Ann-Louise loved her just as much as she loved the other dolls, but the plain fact was that Robin was not alive.

"What!" exclaimed the crow. "Do you mean to say that I was just a lump of black cloth and buttons? A mere rag?"

"Watch it, crow, you don't want to hurt anyone's feelings, do you?" the ragdoll eyed the crow sternly.

"Errr, no...hmmf," he cleared his throat.

Robin

"Anyway, one day last spring Ann-Louise took us all on a picnic up by the orchard. She made little hats of newspaper for us, and she made one for you. Your hat would not stay on your head because of your soft velvet, so she found an old crow feather in the grass and she used it to pin the hat to your head. No sooner had the feather pierced your velvet, but you started cawing and carrying on to beat the band!"

"WHAT! Me, cawing and carrying on! That's absurd!" roared the crow, and he stomped around the room.

"Enough!" warned the ragdoll, "We were all pretty frightened of you at the time, coming alive so suddenly like that, but in time we got used to you and you calmed down some. Now you see you are a regular member of the household, even the dog doesn't bark at you anymore."

Picnic in the Pine Grove

"Hmmm, now that you mention it, I have noticed that he is much quieter than he once was."

"It's not the normal way at all, you know," said the cornhusk doll, "with all these feathers and such. Normally it has to do with the love of a child and so forth, if you know what I mean, or in the case of the ragdoll, I believe that she came into being around the same time as the new electrical system was being installed..."

"Yes, yes, harumph," said the ragdoll quickly. "There was some kind of mix-up involving Bunsen burners and a number of beakers of chemicals in the Captain's laboratory, very scientifical," she looked away.

"So what you are trying to say is that I should not be so afraid of this ape," continued the crow, "that perhaps

"She found an old crow feather in the grass..."

he only needs some getting used to and calming down?"

"Did you ever stop to think that maybe the monkey was trying to help you, silly crow?" replied the ragdoll, "The only one who needs calming down is you!"

The next day was Ann-Louise's birthday, and it was the happiest birthday she ever had. For once her grandfather had not surprised her with one of his dusty curiosities, this year she opened her present to find a beautiful, soft, cotton sock monkey. She hugged him to her cheek and to her delight the monkey started to whisper all about his adventures in the house.

"I'm going to name you Uncle Gabby, because you gab so!" she laughed.

"Come and have some cake!" called her grandmother. "I'm lighting the candles!"

Ann-Louise's Birthday

"Let me first introduce Uncle Gabby to my dollies!" replied Ann-Louise.

The captain looked on and tapped his foot. "Hmmph! Just what this house needs, more magical dolls!" he grumbled.

"Uncle Gabby, I would like to introduce the cornhusk doll," began Ann-Louise, very politely.

"It is a pleasure to meet you, sir," the doll curtsied.

"The joy is mine, to be sure," replied the sock monkey.

"And here are the ragdoll and Robin."

"I am at your service, ladies," bowed Uncle Gabby.

"You are a true gentleman, sir, welcome to our home," answered the ragdoll. Robin said nothing, her hair glistened.

"And this is Mr. Crow," said Ann-Louise.

"I believe that you and I shall be

"I'm going to name you Uncle Gabby!"

very good friends, dear sir," said Uncle Gabby, and the crow wrapped his wings around him and they became true friends on the spot.

Early the next morning, as the dolls were coming down the stairs, the ragdoll asked a question.

"However did you come to life so soon after being sewn together, Uncle Gabby? Do you know, at all?"

"It has something to do with my teeth I think, this coming-to-life business. I know it sounds silly, but I had a dream that I had a real actual tooth in my mouth, and I tell you, I think I really do have a tooth, though of course that is not possible! How could I have any teeth at all, I am only a cloth toy!" The ragdoll and the crow looked nervously at the cornhusk

"I believe that you and I shall be very good friends!"

doll. Teeth, ears, noses and eyes were her favorite subjects. She began to speak.

"You may think it odd, that I have no eyes, that someone so concerned with beauty, indeed, someone so beautiful herself, would have no eyes to see with, but I assure you my dears, I can see you all quite well, though you are yourselves rather plain." The ragdoll and the crow sat down patiently, having heard the story many times. "I once had eyes, and beauties they were, let me tell you, but a problem arose, which was explained to me by the doll doctor, a very learned man, he explained to me the nature of seeing and of light. We see things because of the light which bounces off of them (he demonstrated his theory with an assortment of candles and mirrors, you see). Well, in those days I was something

The ragdoll asked a question.

of an art lover, attending all the gallery openings and visiting the great museums, there are some splendid paintings in the study upstairs, you know. I wanted to fill my eyes with all the beauty in the world, and I tried it by golly! I looked at art, I looked at nature, at night I stared at my grandfather's watch! It had a phosphorescent dial, and it glowed in the dark, you understand. Well, all that light gathered up in my eyes to the point that it started to dribble back out! I had sparkling tears day and night, people thought that I was weeping all of the time, it became quite embarrassing after a while! The doll doctor could find no other answer but to remove my eyes, the most beautiful glass beads! Well, how can one see at all, you ask, without any eyes, but I tell you whether you can believe me

The Cornhusk Doll's Tale

or not, that I can see better now than I ever could! My soul has become so sensitive due to all the looking that I did, that I can practically see right through walls!"

The ragdoll leaned over toward the sock monkey and whispered, "She's actually quite near-sighted, the poor dear, her eyes fell off in an unfortunate accident involving a cotton gin."

The sock monkey put his arm around the crow and drew him close, "I must tell you, Mr. Crow, perhaps I have not been as friendly as I should have been, in fact I have been rather nervous since I came here. I don't want to alarm you, but last night I saw a hideous sort of goblin in the garden. In fact, I would use the same words to describe this monster as you once used to describe me! It has truly put a chill up my back, and

They had heard the tale many times...

if I had hairs on my neck, I tell you, they would be standing on end even now!"

"What!" exclaimed the crow. "Goblins! Here in our own garden? Why that is nonsense, Uncle Gabby, I can assure you that there are no goblins in our garden! The Captain would never allow it, you must be mistaken! Let us go and investigate!"

And with that they ran (or rather tumbled) down the stairs and out the back door.

Ann-Louise and her family lived in a beautiful house, and their garden was lovely to match. Here they grew hollyhocks and foxgloves, pansies and magnolias, and it was from underneath the magnolias that the sock monkey and Mr. Crow cautiously peered.

"Do you see it, Mr. Crow? There by that shallow pool!" The crow looked

"Last night I saw a hideous goblin in the garden!"

about the garden and sure enough, there half hidden by a rosebush, stood a tall horrible figure.

"Gadzooks, Uncle Gabby! It is indeed a Titan from some Greek myth! A real giant, a Colossus!"

They tiptoed forward.

"Well, I wouldn't call it a Titan, Mr. Crow, it is after all, rather small..."

"Small? It is enormous!" he shouted.

"Do not be silly, my dear, if it was any kind of a giant it would surely fall from the shoulder of that statue!"

The crow then realized that he was in fact looking at a statue carved from granite, and there perched upon its shoulder, sat a tiny winged creature.

"Good heavens, Uncle Gabby! Don't tell me that all this time you have been afraid of this gentle fairy!"

"Gadzooks, Uncle Gabby!"

"Fairy! Is that what she is! The way she was flitting about and diving into the pond this afternoon, I could have sworn that she was some kind of a vampire or demon! Oh, how I have played the fool!"

"Diving? I have seen fairies flitting and even fluttering, but I must say that I have never seen them doing any sort of diving! How do you mean, diving?" wondered the crow.

"Why, just this afternoon, she was diving again and again into that pool, grumbling and mumbling! She seemed very disturbed." No sooner had the sock monkey said this, than the fairy swooped off the statue and plunged into the pool, making a tiny but violent splash. Just as suddenly, she sprang out again, and right behind her jumped a huge, fat goldfish, his wide mouth slobbering and snapping!

Right behind her jumped a huge, fat goldfish!

"Heavens! Whatever does she think she is doing?" shrieked the crow. "Everyone knows that that ancient goldfish is the meanest, most vicious creature in these parts!"

"Not everyone, Mr. Crow! I myself have never seen or heard of anything like him! Perhaps, like me, she is new to the scene!" said Uncle Gabby, and he ran to the side of the pool.

"Here, madam, calm yourself!" he gasped. "Not only are these waters full of dangerous monsters, but you have gotten yourself all wet, and that cannot be good for a flying animal such as you! Why, your wings are soaked through and through!"

I don't know if you have ever tried to talk to a fairy, but I can tell you that you won't get very far if you do. They are not only shy creatures, but when they do speak,

The Goldfish

it is with a voice so high and quivering that you cannot understand them at all. You may as well try to talk to a bumblebee.

Nevertheless, the crow started to jabber and wiggle his wings at her. The crow knew a little about fairies, and as she mumbled and griped in her curious high voice, he shouted "WHAT?" and "HOW'S THAT?" now and again. She danced and buzzed around making odd signs and gestures, until finally the crow turned to Uncle Gabby and sighed.

"Why is she so upset, Mr. Crow? What did she say?" asked the sock monkey.

"I haven't the faintest idea what she said, Uncle, but I believe I understand the problem. If you will look down into the pool, you will see a small child's tooth. Through a little scientific thinking, I have come to the conclusion that this is not just

Nevertheless, the crow started to jabber
and wiggle his wings at her.

some ordinary fairy, indeed, she is a Fairy of Teeth, a Tooth Collector!"

"A Tooth Fairy! Goodness, there are so many things in this world that I know nothing about, think of it! A fairy whose special responsibility it is to attend to matters of the human tooth! I am amazed! Does she also concern herself with other types of teeth, those of animals, combs, and such?"

"No, my dear, she takes the teeth of children after they fall out of their mouths," said the crow patiently.

"Fall out! Ye Gads, what are these children up to, that they are knocking themselves so violently in the mouths?!" asked the sock monkey, bewildered. He put his paws to his head.

"Now, now, it is not so dramatic as all that, it has to do with a natural growth

The Tooth Collector

process, quite harmless, I assure you, Uncle Gabby, please don't carry on so. I'll explain it all to you when you are a couple of days old." The crow leaned over the pool's granite edge.

"Now please look into the water, do you see over there, hiding under that lily pad?" Uncle Gabby peered into the pool, eventually he could see a blurry golden object floating in the shadow of the lilies. He had scarcely made out the shape of a large bulging eye, when something buzzed fast by his ear and plunged into the water. It was the fairy, of course, and he could see her down at the bottom of the pool, clutching at the tooth. A streak of gold flashed out from the darkness and the water's surfaced erupted in an enormous splash! The fairy flew into the sky, dropping the tooth, as the bloated

"My, look at her go!"

scaly fish snapped the air, twisted, and tumbled back into the deep!

"My! Look at her go! Such a fearless little sprite!" the sock monkey clapped his soft cotton paws with joy, making no sound. The crow however, was not so joyful, in fact, he was fuming!

"There are times when fearlessness is most certainly NOT a virtue! This foolish fairy is going to get herself gobbled up if she doesn't use some caution, mark my words! It's a very dangerous situation!"

"Perhaps if there was some way we could help her get the tooth..." suggested the sock monkey. He thought for a while. "I have it! We will shoo him away, the old rascal, and give that fairy time to grab her tooth!"

"'Shoo him away' is easy to say, my friend, but that big fish will not be shooed by the likes of us!" replied the crow. "We

A Fearless Sprite

are really nothing more than some sewn-up bits of cotton cloth! He will brush us aside like a couple of old leaves that have fallen from the rose-bush!"

"Courage, Mr. Crow, courage and faith! We will chase him away with a shadow!"

"Why that is absurd, Uncle! Not even a fish would be afraid of a mere shadow!"

"You shall soon see otherwise! Quickly, climb up on my shoulders, my dear!" The crow clambered up and perched on the sock monkey's back. "Hold your wings to your sides and crane your neck out as far as you can, and we will walk over to the pool!"

This they did, and the morning sun cast a shadow on the water. Now, I don't know how much you know about fish, but the one thing besides hooks, bears and

"Quickly, climb up on my shoulders!"

bigger fish that they are afraid of is herons! And if you ever take a toy stuffed crow and set him on top of a sock monkey, you will see that you have formed a shadow puppet that looks just like a big, hungry heron! When that goldfish saw the shadow that Uncle Gabby and Mr. Crow left on the bottom of that pool, he swam as fast as a little scared minnow to the other side of the lily pond and cried for his mommy! The fairy swooped down, grabbed the tooth, and flew off to wherever fairies fly off to, and the sock monkey and the crow cheered her on!

"Well, the tide certainly has changed, my friend!" said the sock monkey, looking proudly at the crow. "When we met yesterday, you were a big scaredy-cat, and just look at you today! Why, you are a regular scare-crow!"

The sun cast a shadow on the water.

"Yes, think of it," exclaimed the crow, "from scaredy-cat to scare-crow, I feel like a new bird! Isn't life grand!"

Ann-Louise woke up later that morning and yawned. She had slept quite late and the sun was shining through her bedroom window. Her birthday the day before had been very exciting, and the cake her grandmother had made for her was delicious: a genuine quadruple decker hazelnut banana chocolate layer cake, with vanilla butter-cream icing! But she remembered that as she was helping herself to a third slice, her tooth had started wiggling, and as though it had a life of its own, it popped right out! She was very alarmed, as you can imagine! Her grandfather had gently explained to her that it was quite all right, and that if

He swam as fast as a little scared minnow!

she put the tooth under her pillow, she would certainly be surprised at what she might find there the next morning.

As she lay in bed remembering what her grandfather had told her, she put her finger in her mouth and felt the hole where her tooth used to be. She threw back the covers and lifted her pillow, and there she found a shiny new dime!

The sunlight shone on Robin's porcelain boots.

She lifted her pillow and there was a shiny new dime!